FOOTBALL CRAZY

COLIN McNAUGHTON

MAMMOTH

for my son Timothy —
welcome to the world.

First published in Great Britain 1980
by William Heinemann Ltd
Published 1989 by Mammoth
an imprint of Reed Books Ltd
Michelin House, 81 Fulham Road, London SW3 6RB
and Auckland, Melbourne, Singapore and Toronto

Reprinted 1990, 1992, 1993 (twice), 1994, 1995,(twice)

Text and illustrations copyright © Colin McNaughton 1980

ISBN 0 7497 0125 0

A CIP catalogue record for this title
is available from the British Library

Produced by Mandarin Offset Ltd
Printed and bound in Hong Kong

Bruno was crazy about football.

The trouble was, he had nobody to play with. He had just moved to the big city with his mum and dad, and he didn't have any friends.

It was Sunday, and he stood at the window and watched a gang of kids playing on some waste ground.

The gang called themselves Tex's Tigers.
Bruno thought they were terrific.

He watched Tex
flick the ball to Patch

and Patch nod it over to Ginger

and Ginger backheel it
up to Roberto

and Roberto head it towards the goal,
where it was beautifully saved by Winston.
Bruno longed to join in.

"Why don't you go and play with those children?" asked
his mum.

"I don't know them. They wouldn't want me," said
Bruno.

"Nonsense," said his mum. "You're a good footballer.
You run outside and ask them."

Bruno was shy, but at last he plucked up his courage and
crossed the street to the waste ground.

"Hey, can I come and play with you?" he called to the gang.

Tex's Tigers climbed the fence and looked down on him.

"Play?" scowled Roberto. "We're not playing. We're training."

"Saturday's the big match," Ginger explained. "We're playing Leroy's Lions. They're our deadliest rivals."

"Couldn't I train with you?" begged Bruno.

The gang looked at each other.

"Shall we let him?" asked Winston.

"Okay," said Tex. "Let's see what you can do."

Bruno was hopeless. He slipped, he tripped, he fluffed and he duffed. He bumped into everyone.

"It's just that I'm out of practice," he told them.

"Let's put him in goal," said Winston. "He'll be out of harm's way there."

Once Bruno got used to being in goal, he began to enjoy himself.

After a tricky save Winston said, "Not bad. Not bad at all." Bruno beamed with pride.

When they had finished training, the Tigers made plans for
the big match. Tex talked of sweepers and strikers and
midfield generals. Patch and Winston discussed forwards
and half backs and full backs and wingers. Ginger and
Roberto argued about inside rights and offside traps,
man-to-man marking and dead ball situations.

"Can I be in the team?" asked Bruno timidly.

The gang groaned, and Tex said kindly, "'Fraid not,
Bruno. It's five-a-side and we've got five already."

Bruno looked crestfallen.

"I suppose you could be the substitute," Tex went on. "After all," he said to the others, "he's a pretty good goalkeeper, and if someone was injured he could go in goal. And Winston, you could take the injured player's place."

"That's okay by me," said Winston.

"But you'll have to do a lot better than you did today," said Tex. "We can't afford any mistakes on Saturday."

"Oh, thank you," cried Bruno. "Don't worry, I won't let you down."

Bruno trained hard. He was determined to improve.
He practised every day after school.

On Monday it was running.

On Tuesday it was heading.

On Wednesday it was passing.

On Thursday it was dribbling

and on Friday it was scoring goals.

Then it was Saturday, the day of the match. The night before, Bruno's dreams were full of football.

"It's no fun being the substitute," he sighed at breakfast. "I do wish I was in the team."

"Who says you won't be?" said his dad. "You never know what might happen. Football's a crazy game."

"We'll be there to cheer you on, just in case you get a chance to play," said his mum.

As kick-off time grew near, Tex's Tigers gathered in the gang hut.

"Here you are, Bruno, you can wear this," said Patch, tossing him the team's spare football strip. It looked much too big for him, but Bruno didn't mind. He was proud to wear the colours of Tex's Tigers.

Bruno was still dressing when Tex said, "Come on, time to go."

"But I'm not ready," said Bruno.

"Never mind," said Tex. "You stay here in case we need you." And the Tigers trooped out onto the pitch.

A cheer went up from the crowd. Leroy's Lions were out there already, warming up. Bruno finished putting on his boots and settled down to watch from the tiny gang hut window.

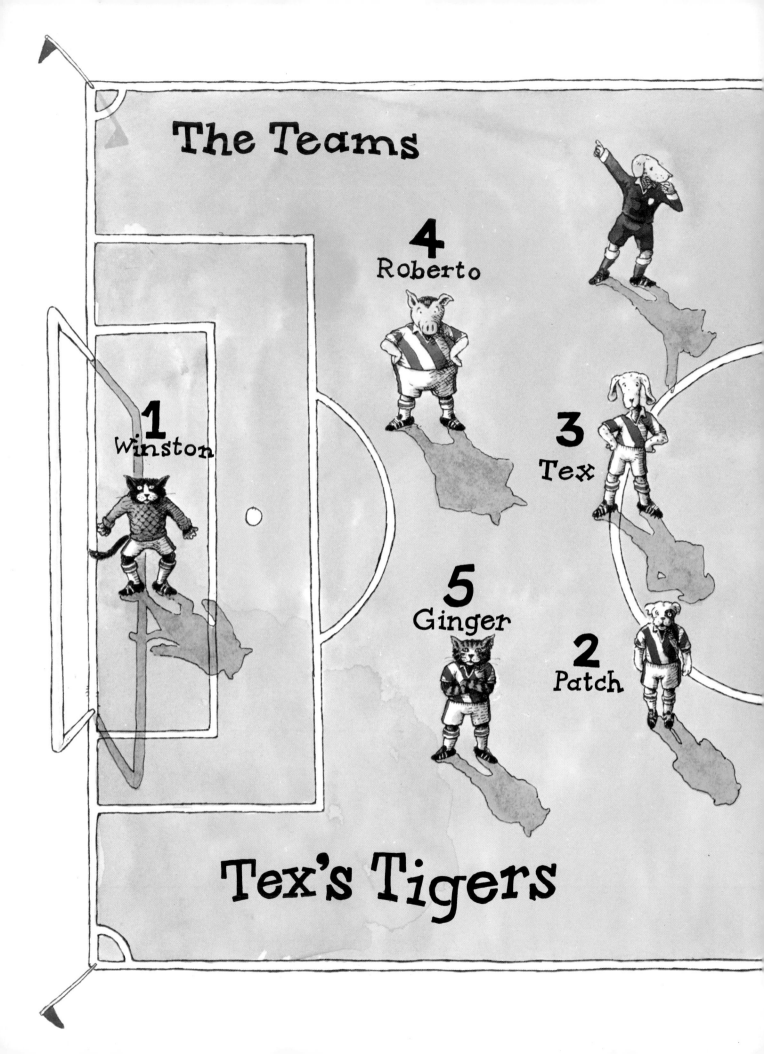

The Teams

4 Roberto

1 Winston

3 Tex

5 Ginger

2 Patch

Tex's Tigers

The referee blew his whistle. They were off! The pace was
fast and furious and the play swung from one end to the other.

The Tigers scored first.

Then the Lions equalized.

What a goal! The Lions take the lead.

Oh no, they've scored again! The Tigers are 3–1 down.

Tex looks worried.   So does Bruno.

The Tigers pull one back. HOORAY!

Come on, Tigers, you can do it! Oh, hard luck.

Yes, it's there. What a goal! 3 goals each.

Tigers, Tigers, Tigers, *oooh!*

Lions, Lions, Lions, *aaah!*

FOUL! Roberto is brought down.
IT'S A PENALTY TO TEX'S TIGERS!!!

Poor Roberto was knocked out and had to be carried off.

"Come on, Bruno!" shouted Tex. "You're on! Get in goal!"

It was Bruno's big chance. He took a deep breath and trotted onto the pitch. Hoots of laughter greeted him. Well, he did look a little odd in his huge shorts and boots.

Bruno was just thinking how unfair it was when the referee signalled for the penalty to be taken. "I'll show them!" said Bruno to himself. "They won't laugh at me when I score a goal!"

And he ran the full length of the pitch and kicked the ball as hard as he could . . .

. . . right out of the stadium.

The Lions' fans went wild, laughing and jeering.

The Tigers' fans went wild, booing and howling.

"Now look what you've done!" yelled Tex. "Get back in goal. You've probably lost the match for us."

Bruno was ashamed of himself, but there was no time to brood. The Lions mounted one attack after another. No one was laughing at Bruno now, as he pulled off a string of great saves.

But then Bruno made a dreadful mistake.

He dived for the ball at Leroy's feet, missed it and sent Leroy sprawling. There were only two minutes to go and Bruno had given away a penalty. If Leroy scored, the Lions would win the match and it would all be Bruno's fault.

He just had to save it.

Bruno felt tiny. The goal seemed huge. The crowd was silent. Tex and his Tigers turned away. They couldn't watch. They knew they were beaten. Leroy had never missed a penalty in his life.

The whistle blew. Would he? Could he?

Had he?   Yes, he had – BRUNO HAD SAVED IT!!!

A roar went up from the crowd, but Bruno wasn't finished yet. He kicked the ball high, high in the air, right over the head of the Lions' goalkeeper, who had come out from his goal to watch the penalty, and into the back of the net.

There was a stunned silence, then the crowd went wild. The referee blew his whistle and it was all over. Thanks to Bruno, Tex's Tigers had beaten Leroy's Lions by 4 goals to 3.

"Good old Bruno!" shouted Tex. "You're a hero!"

"Bruno, Bruno, Bruno," chanted the crowd, and they carried him around the ground on a lap of honour.

Bruno saw his mum and dad waving, and he waved back. They were so proud of him.

"Can I be sub in the next match, Tex?" asked Bruno.

"You bet," said Tex. "We couldn't do without you."

And that just about made Bruno's day.